COUNTDOWN TO KINDERGARTEN

by

Alison McGhee

Pictures by

Harry Bliss

Silver Whistle • Harcourt, Inc.
San Diego   New York   London

www.HarcourtBooks.com

Silver Whistle is a trademark of Harcourt, Inc.,
registered in the United States of America and/or other jurisdictions.

Library of Congress Cataloging-in-Publication Data
McGhee, Alison, 1960–
Countdown to kindergarten/Alison McGhee; pictures by Harry Bliss.
p.   cm.
"Silver Whistle."
Summary: Ten days before the start of kindergarten,
a pre-kindergartner cannot tie her shoes by herself and fears the worst.
[1. Fear—Fiction.   2. Kindergarten—Fiction.   3. First day of school—
Fiction.   4. Schools—Fiction.]   I. Bliss, Harry, 1964–, ill.   II. Title.
PZ7.M4786475Co   2002
[E]—dc21   2001004648
ISBN 0-15-202516-2

G H

Manufactured in China

The pictures in this book were done in black ink
and watercolor on Arches 90 lb. watercolor paper.
The display lettering was created by Harry Bliss.
The text type was hand lettered by Paul Colin.
Color separations by Bright Arts Ltd., Hong Kong
Manufactured by South China Printing Company, Ltd., China
This book was printed on totally chlorine-free Nymolla Matte Art paper.
Production supervision by Sandra Grebenar and Ginger Boyer
Designed by Suzanne Fridley

For Devon O'Brien
—A. M.

For Carol Dolnick
—H. B.

Rule #3: You're not allowed to bring any stuffed animals.

Rule #2: You're not allowed to bring your cat.

Rule #1: You have to know how to tie your shoes. By yourself. You're not allowed to ask for help. Ever.

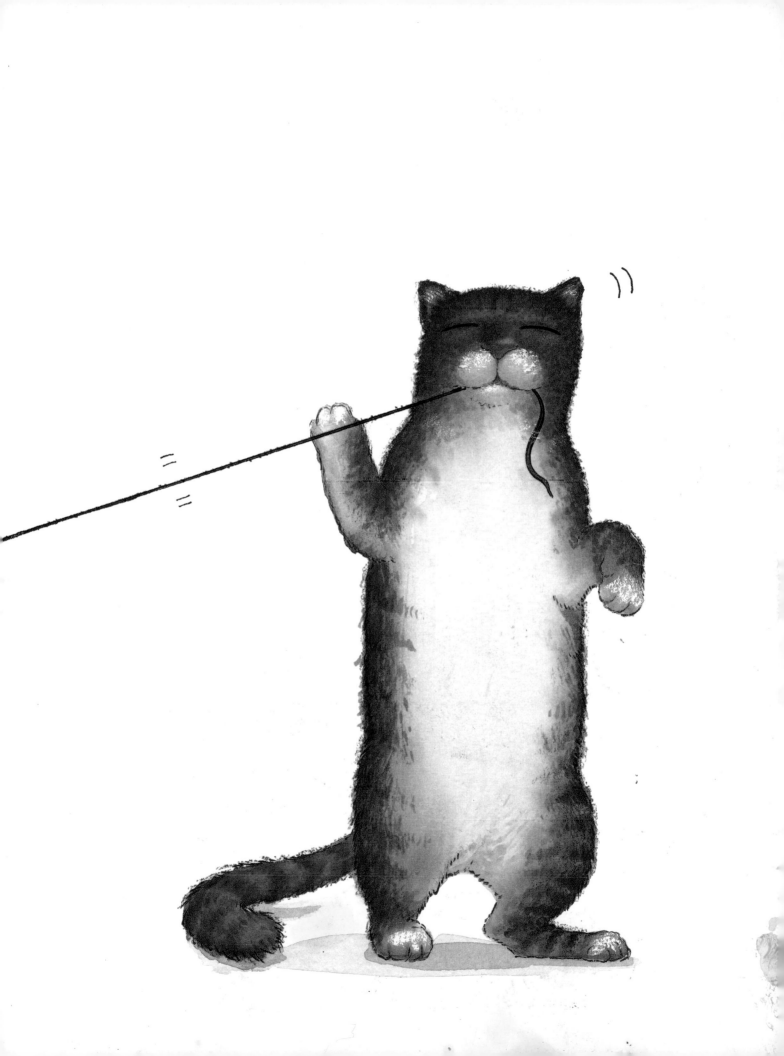

NINE DAYS BEFORE KINDERGARTEN.

This isn't getting any easier.

EIGHT DAYS BEFORE KINDERGARTEN.

YUCK!

YUCKY PUDDLE

Even the rain puddle is out to get me.

I know…I'll pull the laces out. Imagine what could happen if I left them in…

I know…I'll throw them out.

Dad says a lot of five-year-olds don't know how to tie. I guess he hasn't heard Kindergarten Rule #1.

Dad practices with me.

Look at his knot. Just the way he showed me.

Puddy, here's your lunch.

LATER THAT DAY...

Repeat after me: Bowls are for cat food, shoes are for your feet.

Mom says a lot of five-year-olds don't know how to tie.
I guess *she* doesn't know about Rule #1, either.

I wonder if you can show up at kindergarten wearing your baby shoes.

Okay. Back to my bedroom for more practice.

THREE DAYS BEFORE KINDERGARTEN.

Loop, pull around, poke, and pull.

Dad is so nice. He even bought me new laces. That should help.

Snack time for Puddy.

LATER THAT DAY...

TWO DAYS BEFORE KINDERGARTEN.

My parents are taking me out for my favorite dinner—spaghetti—to celebrate the start of school. I don't see anything to celebrate.

How's your bowl of shoelaces—I mean spaghetti?

Dad says, "Don't worry, sweetie. It just takes time." But kindergarten starts in two days! What if I have to wear a sign that says…

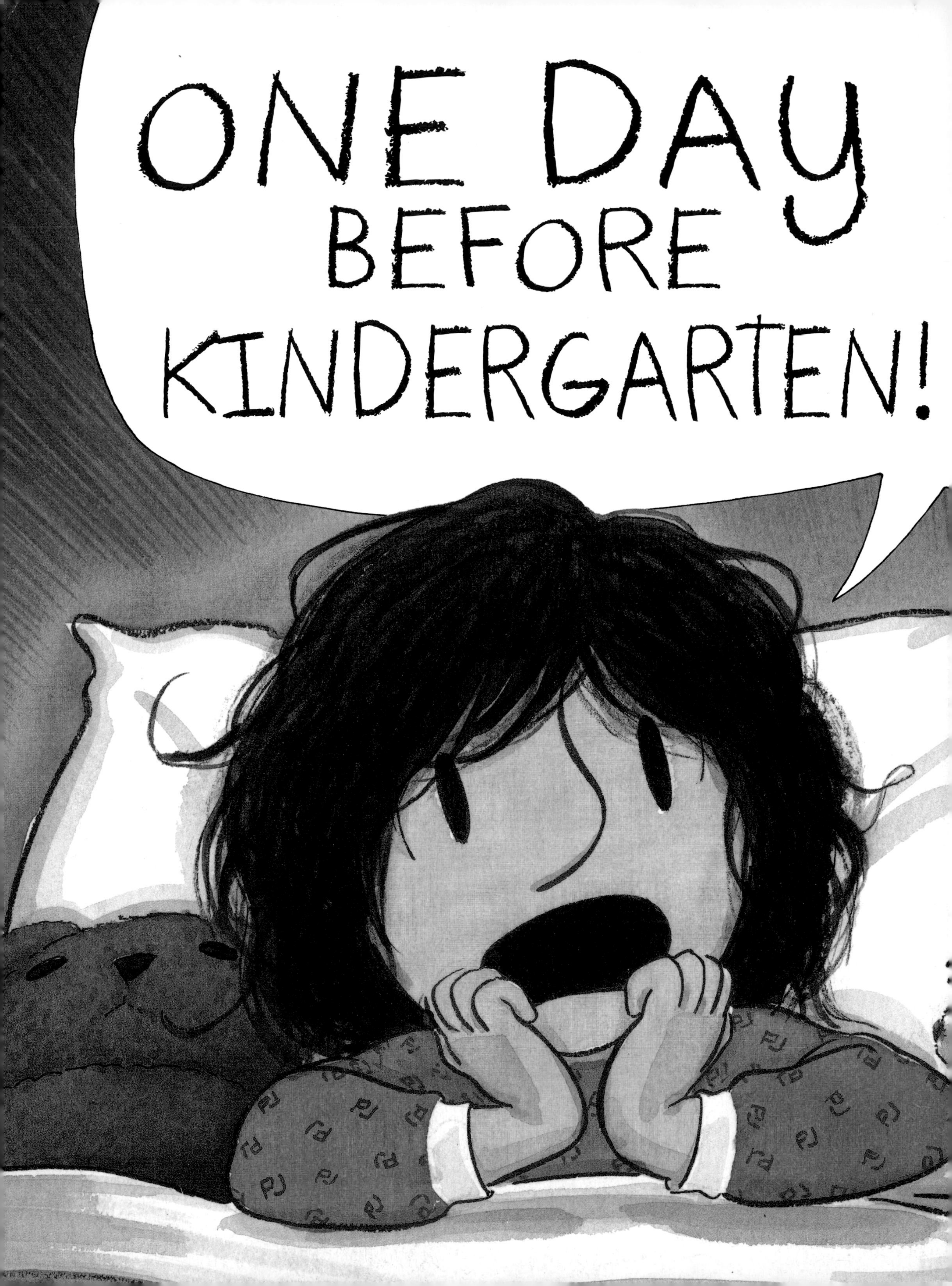
ONE DAY BEFORE KINDERGARTEN!

FIRST DAY OF KINDERGARTEN.

LATER THAT MORNING...

MONDAY: SHOE TYING
(TEACHER CAN HELP)

TUESDAY: STUFFED ANIMAL
DAY

WEDNESDAY: COUNTING
BACKWARDS FROM TEN

PATIENCE
A SELF HELP
MANUAL.
BY
MISTER ROGERS
PHD BOB ROSS

I guess I'm not in such big trouble after all.